First U.S. Edition   1   2   3   4   5   6   7   8   9   10

Library of Congress Cataloging in Publication Data
McAllister, Angela. The snow angel / by Angela McAllister ;
illustrations by Claire Fletcher.
p.   cm.   Summary: Elsa thinks her little brother imagines seeing a
snow angel until she meets the angel herself.
ISBN 0-688-04569-3   [1. Snow-Fiction.   2. Angels—Fiction.   3. Brothers and
sisters—Fiction.]   I. Fletcher, Claire, ill.   II. Title.
PZ7.M47825So   1993   [E]—dc20   92-44155   CIP   AC

The Snow Angel

BY ANGELA McALLISTER
ILLUSTRATED BY CLAIRE FLETCHER

LOTHROP, LEE & SHEPARD BOOKS

NEW YORK

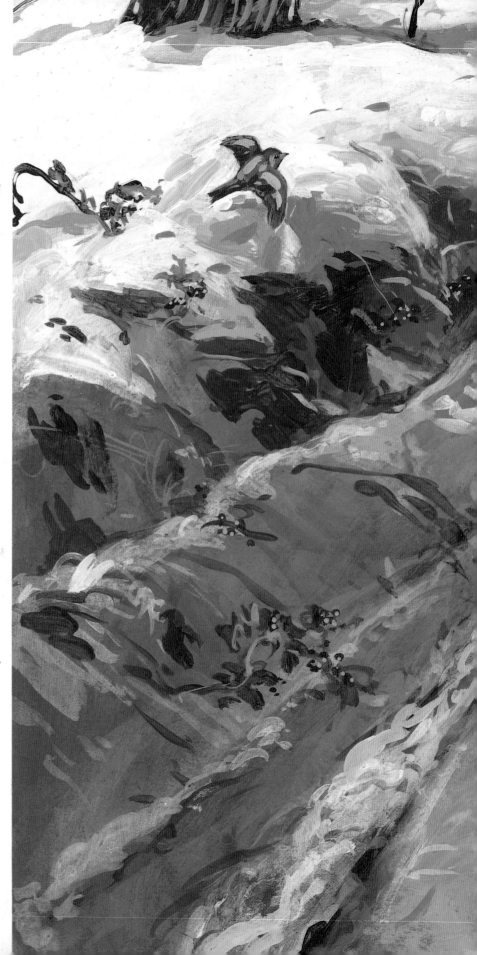

$\mathcal{S}$ecretly the snow had
fallen all night long.
By morning the world was
white. Elsa made Giant
footprints to the frozen
pond, she built snow
castles, and she slid
down the sliding slope.

*Then, in her secret place,
she lay on the
blanket of snow and
spread her arms like
wings.*

"This is where a snow angel slept," she told her little brother.

That Jack—he always thought her tales were true. "I wish I could see a snow angel," he sighed, "more than anything in the whole world."

The next morning Jack was very excited. "I saw her!" he told Elsa. "Last night I saw the snow angel sweep away the snowdrifts, and she gave me a wish, and I rode all night on a giant rabbit, and it's true, I really did!"

But Elsa just smiled. That Jack was always dreaming.

The next morning Jack was even more excited. "The snow angel came again!" he said. "She melted the ice with her breath, and she gave me a wish, and all the fish could fly, even that old whiskery one, and I saw it, Elsa, I really saw it!"

But Elsa just smiled. That Jack was always telling stories.

The next morning Jack was still more excited. "The swinging tree was so covered with snow it almost crashed through my window, but the snow angel blew it all away, and she gave me a wish, and all the icicles were made of sugar, and I ate a hundred. I really really did!"

But Elsa just smiled. That Jack was a good pretender.

That night a fresh snowfall covered Elsa's Giant footprints and her castles. But when she went back to her secret place, an angel's shape still glistened in the snow. Were those the wings she had made?

Carefully, Elsa lay down
in the angel's shape. It
was not her size. She
thought about Jack. Then
she shut her eyes and made
a wish. And when she sat
up, snow wings had
begun to grow. Just
little snow buds at first.
Then long, white
feathers unfolded on her
back and lifted her into
the air.

Up and up Elsa flew. She
danced on treetops. She
raced with birds. Then
she swooped down to skim
above the stepping stream.
And there, half–hidden
behind a tree trunk,
someone was waiting
for her.

All morning Elsa flew with the snow angel—in and out of shadows, high over the rooftops—until the sun began to melt her wings. One last swoop, then Elsa softly fell to earth.

Jack met her at the sliding slope. "I didn't see a snow angel last night," he said, "but I saw two this morning!"

Elsa looked up through the snowflakes and laughed. Maybe that Jack knew a true thing after all.